ANNA LINDWASSER

DEAR ALIEN

WEST 44 BOOKS™

Please visit our website, www.west44books.com.
For a free color catalog of all our high-quality books, call toll free 1-800-398-2504.

Cataloging-in-Publication Data

Names: Lindwasser, Anna.
Title: Dear alien / Anna Lindwasser.
Description: Buffalo, NY : West 44, 2027. | Series: West 44 YA verse
Identifiers: ISBN 9781978598591 (pbk.) | ISBN 9781978598584 (library bound) | ISBN 9781978598607 (ebook)
Subjects: LCSH: Space colonies--Fiction. | Friendship--Fiction. | Pen pals--Fiction. | Earth (Planet)--Fiction. | Mars (Planet)--Fiction.
Classification: LCC PZ7.1.L563 De 2027 | DDC [F]--dc23

First Edition

Published in 2027 by
Enslow Publishing
2544 Clinton Street
Buffalo, NY 14224

Editor: Caitie McAneney
Designer: Tanya Dellaccio Keeney

Photo Credits: Cover (space) CeltStudio/Shutterstock.com.

Printed in the United States of America

CPSIA compliance information: Batch #CS27W44: For further information contact Enslow Publishing LLC at 1-800-398-2504.

To all the people on Earth
who make this place worth protecting.

RAINY

FIRST-GENERATION MARTIANS

I am one of the
first human beings
born on Mars.

There are only about
30 of us.

Other kids were born on Earth
and traveled here.

Besides us,
there are about
100 adults.

We all live crowded
together under
a gigantic dome.

For better or worse,
we only have
each other.

THE MARS PROGRAM

My mom says
they're working
on making Martian air
breathable for
humans. But
they aren't quite
there yet.

She says
        they brought over
        too many wealthy
        space tourists
        and not enough
        scientists and
        engineers.

Mom is a
botanist. It's her
job to set up
an agricultural system.

She
always wrinkles
her nose when
she talks about
the rich people who
bought their way onto
the shuttle.

But they’re the ones
who had more kids.

So if I want to have friends,
I can’t be seen
agreeing with her.

I DON'T KNOW WHAT I THINK

I do know
that with few
other teenagers
around, I can't
afford to make
any of them
hate me.

(Even though
most days
I already think
they hate me.)

EARTH PEN PALS

In school, Ms. Nazarian says,
"I have a surprise
for you!"

Everyone groans.

Last time Ms. Nazarian
had a surprise
for us, we had to
help build a
warehouse.

"Those of you
who were born
on Earth have
few memories
of it. Those of you
who were born
here have none.

But you
are human.

Earth is your
heritage.

We
don't want you
to forget where
you come from."

Electra has bright
yellow hair that matches
her name. She says,
"Are we doing another
Earth study unit?
B O R I N G."

"Not boring," I mumble.

Electra doesn't hear me.
No one ever does.

"You could say that,"
says Ms. Nazarian.
"But it'll be a little
more interactive.

Our school has
partnered with
the Manhattan School
for Space Exploration.

It's an Earth school
attended by the children
of those who made
it possible for us
to come to Mars.

They want to learn
about life on Mars.

And you can learn about life on Earth."

Electra rolls her eyes. "I don't *care* about life on Earth."

"That attitude is exactly why you need to learn more about it. Through your new pen pal, you'll learn about a new way of life. And you might also make a new friend."

A NEW FRIEND

I don't really make
friends.

But I learn that
my pen pal
is Neptune Rose.

She has such
a pretty name.

I'm already interested.

MOST OF OUR NEW PEN PALS

have space-themed names.

Snowy has Venus.
Cloudan has Cosmos.
And Electra has Milkiwei.

Ms. Nazarian says
people on Earth
think space
represents hope
for humanity's
continued future.

So, that's the deal with
the space names.

It's similar to
the reason
most of us
are named after
natural features
on Earth.

The beloved
place our
parents left
behind.

I HAVE NEVER BEEN TO EARTH

So I'm not sure
what parts of Martian living
would be interesting
to someone from there.

Earth has a *much*
longer history.
At least when
it comes to humans.

Martian bacteria
has been around
for millions of years.

There might have
been plants.

Maybe even
sentient life
before us.

But not humans.

We're the first.

We have no history
to report.

We can't
even explore
the whole planet.
The air outside
of our dome
is 95 percent carbon dioxide.

Earth seems
so much more
exciting.

What can I tell
Neptune
that won't
bore her?

NEPTUNE

THE TEACHER'S WARNING

My classmates
and I start
comparing notes
on our new
pen pals.

Then Mr. Okafor
speaks:
"I know that you're
all excited to
talk to your
pen pals," he says.
"But there are
a few ground rules."

Everyone groans.

"First, the obvious.
You're allowed
to be yourselves.
But there are limits.
I don't want to
hear about
any of you
bullying those
Mars kids."

“We’re not going
to bully them!”
shouts Milkiwei.
“We’re the *nicest
people ever.*”

“You’d better be.
You’re representing
Earth to people
who have never
experienced it
before. So you
have to make
a good impression.”

“What do you
think makes
a good impression?”
I ask.

Mr. Okafor
takes a deep
breath. It’s like
he can tell that we’re
not going to like what
he says next.

DON'T BE NEGATIVE

Mr. Okafor says,
"I know that
some of you have
complaints
about life here.

Fair ones.

But we don't
want you to
focus on the
negative when
you're talking
to your pen pals.

We want them
to see the
positive things
about Earth.

If everything
goes well,
Mars will
become a
second home
for humankind.

If we make
life on Earth
look awful,
it will make
the people of
Earth look
just as bad."

I raise my hand.

"Yes, Neptune?"

"So we're supposed to
lie to them?
What's the point in
talking to them
at all if we
can't be honest?"

"I didn't say to lie.
Just stay focused
on the positive.
For example, instead
of telling them
about the hurricane
last month, you
could tell them
about our
recent school trip
to the Metropolitan
Museum of Art."

I grind my teeth.
"But a lot of things
are bad! Why shouldn't
we be honest about it?"

I wish I had my camera right now
to record the garbage
coming out of his mouth.

"Because many
of the problems
we have on Earth
will be impossible
for them to understand.

There has never been
a war on Mars. There
has never been a
pandemic. They
haven't even
experienced
bad weather.

By the time
you get done
explaining
everything bad about
Earth, they'll
have lost interest.

Focus on getting
to know them."

GOOD THINGS?

There *are*
good things about
life on Earth. But
I can't think of
any of them.

I *do* remember the art museum.

How some of my classmates
tried to imitate the poses
of the Greek statues.

But that's not all I remember.

I remember a lady
standing on the
subway platform.
Begging for change.

I remember
a sudden hard rain
starting to flood the
subway station.

And I remember hiding
in the bathroom
at the museum.

Having a panic attack
because the art
reminded me of my brother,
the best artist I knew.
And the fact
that he was dead.

I remember
lying in bed
that night,
trying to breathe.
Battling a migraine I
got from the
heat and the
rain and the
stress of the day.

MIGRAINES

My head always
hurts. At least
a little bit.

When I'm stressed
or tired or overheated,
it turns into a migraine.

Sometimes I can
get through
them. I wear
sunglasses to
stop bright lights
from making them
worse. Sometimes
the medication
works.

But sometimes
it knocks me out.

I'm stuck in bed
for hours—or
days. I turn
off the lights
and keep the
blackout
curtains closed.

I only get up
to throw up
in the bathroom.

The hotter it gets
around here,
the more days
I have like that.

RAINY

CLOUDAN SAYS I SHOULD START BY

telling Neptune
about myself. That's
what he's doing with his
partner, a freckled boy
named Cosmos.

I don't think
Neptune will
want to know
about me.

I'm not very interesting.
But I'll try.

WE USE A SPECIAL TERMINAL

that connects us
to Earth's internet.

We only have a few
of them in the
whole dome.

One belongs to
the mayor. Some of the
celebrities have
private ones
that let them
livestream their
Mars experience
to their fans.

Another one
is in Science Hall
for the engineers
and scientists.

And our school
has two.

WHEN MY TIME SLOT ARRIVES

I sit down in
the terminal booth.
I upload
the photo of myself
I hate the least.

In most photos, it
looks like my
eyes are my
only facial feature.
They're too big.

Most of the time,
I try to hide
behind my hair.

But in this photo,
my shoulder-length
brown hair is
pulled back into
a half ponytail.

And I'm wearing
my favorite outfit—
a striped purple-and-white dress
my mom brought
from Earth.

I'm not pretty.
But in this picture,
I think I look . . . friendly?

NEPTUNE'S PROFILE

has a photo too.
She's *beautiful.*

Her hair is brown
like mine, but
wavy. The
tips are
dyed blue.
It's almost the
same color as
her eyes.

She's wearing
a black shirt
with glittery
threads
that look
like veins.

She has earrings
shaped like
the planet
she's named for.

Silver circles
look like half-moons
under her eyes.

I hope
she won't
think I'm
too ugly
and boring
to talk to.

I flex my fingers
and start typing.

DEAR NEPTUNE ROSE,

My name is Rainy Donovan.
I'm a student
at Mars Academy. I'm 16.

The high school has only one teacher.
So I'm in the same class as
my little sister Snowy. She's 13.

She doesn't like me very much.

Most people don't. I won't
blame you if you don't either.

Anyway.

My parents are both
scientists. My mom
works in a greenhouse. She
makes sure we can
grow enough food for the
community. Long term, she wants
to grow food outside the dome.

We live in a dome, by the way.
Because Mars doesn't have
oxygen. Plus, the gravity is
really different.

My dad keeps
oxygen levels inside
the dome human friendly.

It's weird to think
that my parents have
such huge
responsibilities.
All I do is
go to school.
Someday I'll have a job
that helps the dome,
but I'm not sure
what that will be.

I'm not sure
what else
to say.

I'm looking forward
to hearing
about your life
on Earth.

Sincerely,
Rainy Donovan

AFTER SCHOOL

We go to a taco truck.

I get chorizo tacos
and Andromeda gets
shrimp.

It's been
a while since
we've hung out.

We used to spend hours
making videos
about anything and everything—
documentaries following potato bugs
or skateboarders at the park.

I haven't really
wanted to hang
out with anyone
lately. Not since
my brother died.

But Andromeda
told me she
needed tacos
or she would
explode.

We walk to
Central Park
and find somewhere
to sit down.

"Did you get your
first letter from
Mars?" asks Andromeda.

"Yeah, from this
girl named Rainy," I say.
"A bit heavy on the
self-esteem issues."

"Surprising coming from
a uber-privileged Mars kid,"
Andromeda laughs.
"Looks like
nobody gave her
the 'don't be negative'
lecture."

"Well, she wasn't
trying to make
Mars sound bad.
But she said most
people don't like her."

"Awkward."

"Yeah. She said her
little sister doesn't
like her either."

"Oh . . . that must
have felt weird
to hear. You
basically ripped
my head off
after I told you
I got into a fight
with my brother."

"Sorry about that."
I take a bite of my taco.

"It's okay. I'd probably
be kind of a jerk too
if my brother died.
Are you going to
tell your pen pal
what happened to him?"

"I don't know.
Especially if
we're not allowed
to tell the truth
about our lives."

But I can't *not* talk
about Mercury's death.
It's all I can think about.

DEAR RAINY,

It's nice to meet you.
It is. Don't just assume
that people won't like you,
okay? You're probably
great.

Anyway, even if I end up
not liking you,
we have to do this
for school. So,
let's talk.

The whole
"people living on Mars" thing
has always felt more
like a dream than
something that
actually happens.

I don't know how
you separate
humans from Earth.

You may as well
be an alien. But I guess
you probably think
I'm an alien too.

You said you wanted
to learn about my
life on Earth.
My parents also have
huge responsibilities.
My mom helps
manage communication
between Earth and Mars.

Without her,
you guys wouldn't
be able to use
Earth's internet. We
wouldn't be
able to write
to each other.

My dad helped design
the dome that your dad
maintains.

I'm 15.

My brother would be
18 if he were still
alive.

That's a sad story
you probably don't care about.

But I have about 1,000
questions I want to ask.

Here's one: do you
have elections on Mars?

Write back soon.
I'm really bored
over here. Your
letter was the
highlight of
my day.

Your Friendly Neighborhood Alien,
Neptune

HOW CAN SHE BE BORED?

She lives on *Earth*.
A whole planet
covered with life.
I bet she's
seen a jaguar.
I bet she's been
on a roller coaster.
I bet she's seen
the ocean. Maybe
even swum in it.
Her food is *real* and varied,
not freeze-dried
from Earth
or grown in a small greenhouse.

She can
go to museums
and see
amazing works
of art *in person*.

But maybe
it doesn't matter
what her world
is like.

Her brother is
dead.
Maybe
she's too
depressed to
enjoy what
Earth
has to offer.

DEAR FRIENDLY NEIGHBORHOOD ALIEN,

You're right—I guess
we're *both* aliens.

We usually
call ourselves Martians.
We call you Earthians.
But my parents
say that's not what
people on Earth
call themselves.

What do you
call yourselves?

Please don't
feel bad about
telling me about
your brother. I
don't know how
we could become
friends if you kept
something so
important
to yourself.

I don't have the
best social skills.

I don't understand
most people. Or
maybe they don't
understand me.

Anyway,
I can't promise
to know the
right thing to say.
But I can promise
to listen.

You can also
ask me anything
you want about
Mars. I'm
not very
smart, but
I can try
to answer.

About elections:
yes, we have them,
but so far, we only
have one politician.

Her name is
Destiny Redding—
I'm sure you know her
as the famous pop singer
and movie star.

She made
enough money
to buy a ticket
to Mars.

Now we call her
the Dome Mayor.

I don't know
her very well.
But her son
Forest spends
a lot of time
in the greenhouse
with my mom.

He's weird—
last time I tried
to say hello,
he just beeped
at me. Like a robot.

But he knows a lot
of fun facts about bugs.

Did you know that
fruit flies were
the first living thing
to enter outer space?

Sorry, you
asked about
voting, not Forest.

I think the adults
voted for Dome Mayor Redding.
But I don't think
there was any
competition.

Your Anxious Alien Friend,
Rainy Donovan

NEPTUNE

DEAR ALIEN WHO IS ABOUT TO HEAR SOMETHING SAD,

If I tell you about
my brother's death,
I'll have to tell you
about life on Earth.

I don't know
what you're
learning about us
at Mars Academy.

I'm guessing you're
mostly learning
about the fun stuff.

My teacher says
we're not supposed
to talk about what
Earth is *really* like.

But I don't think
anyone is reading
the letters.

And I'm not great
with lying.

If you don't
want to know, stop
reading now.

Still there?

Okay.

My brother,
Mercury,
had really
bad asthma.

Our polluted air
damaged his
lungs when
he was a baby.

He wasn't
supposed to
go outside
without
a respirator.

He wasn't
supposed to
go out at all
when the air
quality was bad.
Or when the
temperature
went into
the 90s or 100s.

He definitely
wasn't supposed
to spend the
whole day
outside
working on
a mural.

But the air quality
dipped midway
through the day.

I was recording it on video.
I was going to make this
whole reel about his mural process.
I knew he'd be famous
one day.
He was *that* talented.

But then he collapsed.

He died
from a combination
of asthma and
heatstroke.

This kind of thing
happens all the time
on Earth. The
environment is
killing us.

And Mercury never finished
his mural.
He was so close.

It is still the most
beautiful thing
I've ever seen.
I'm not just saying that
because it's a picture of me
or because my brother is dead.
I mean it. It's amazing.

But I wish he never
started it.
Then maybe
he would still
be alive.

Sorry to
be
such a
downer.

I'll send you
a picture
of the mural
to make up
for it.

Your depressing alien friend,
Neptune

I OPEN UP THE IMAGE

The mural is
beautiful.

A wavy-haired girl
wears a dress
with a map of
Earth on it.

She reaches
toward
a swirl of red
and orange
representing
Mars.

There's
writing at
the bottom.

It says,
"Save our children.
Open up the
Mars Program."

So it wasn't just
a beautiful image.

It was created
to accomplish
something.

But what did
it mean to
open up
the Mars Program?

What message
did Mercury
want to spread?

What was so
important that
he spent hours
painting in the
blazing heat?

That he kept
painting
even though
it was killing him?

I want to
understand.

DEAR NEPTUNE,

The mural is beautiful.
Your brother
must have really loved you
to paint such a wonderful
picture of you.

But it seems like
there was
another message
he wanted to send.

I don't want to
make assumptions.
Maybe it was a metaphor.

But it seems like
he wanted to
leave Earth—or
for you to
leave Earth?

Also, this might be a
weird question, but
were you always proud
of your brother's talent?
Or were you ever . . .
jealous of it?

Sincerely,
Rainy Donovan

NEPTUNE

HEY RAINY,

Yes, my brother
wanted us
to go to Mars.

Earth is dangerous.
We've had like 12
different pandemics
since I was born.
Deadly hurricanes at least
once a month.
Extreme heat—
seriously, right now
it's 115 degrees
and it's only May.

When it's hot, I get migraines so bad
I can't do anything.
I'll be lucky
just to finish high school
at this rate.

I'm scared of
what's going to happen
when summer comes.

And that's just
the natural world.
If you add
the awful things
that people do, it's
even worse.

So, Mercury wanted
us to be safe.

But also, he
thought that
it was a chance
to start society
all over again.

To do things
right this time.
But unless your parents
are hired to work on-site
on the Mars Colony,
or you're rich enough
to tag along, it's
impossible.

We're stuck here
waiting for
the next hurricane
to destroy our
home.

Or the next
plague to
take us out.

It’s not even
that bad here
compared to
other parts
of the world.

I read that
the temperature
gets into
the 130s
in India.

I think you’re
really lucky
to have been
born somewhere
that humans
haven’t
ruined yet.

Your downer alien friend,
Neptune

I FIND MOM IN THE GREENHOUSE

tending to a patch of kale.

"This is growing
beautifully," she says.

She wipes sweat
from her forehead.
"You'll need to
help me think
of some creative ways
to prepare kale.
We're going to be
eating a lot of it this week."

"Could we make
a cake out of it?" I ask.

"Probably not. The
sugar cane I tried
to grow didn't work out."

"Oh, okay."
I'm a little sad about this.
I love the idea of cake.

I try to think of another use for kale. I can't. Maybe later I should ask Neptune about Earth recipes.

ACTING CLASS

Mr. Wu claps his hands.
"That was *brilliant*,
Snowy! You
had me convinced
that you were
actually a fairy
queen!"

My sister grins
at Mr. Wu.
Snowy pushes her
white hair
behind her ear.
She's always so good
at everything.

"Thank you, Mr. Wu,"
she says, smiling at him.
Slightly starstruck, even now.

Back on Earth,
Lance Wu was one of the
most famous
actors alive.

I go to school with his kids:
Cloudan, Stratta, and Skylar.

They're a celebrity family.

We don't have the
technology or the staff
to make movies. These
days, he teaches
acting and public speaking workshops
at the school.

I know he means well.
But I hate the
workshops. You
either do things
that make other people
look at you
or you refuse.

Refusing
also makes people
look at you.

I'm dreading our
final group project
at the end of the year.

Mr. Wu says we need to
use our presentation skills.

Great.

MR. WU ACTS OUT A MONOLOGUE

from one of his Earth movies.

My mom once
said that he "struts like
a peacock." But
I don't know what
a peacock is.

Snowy, Electra, and
Skylar all crowd
around him,
wide-eyed.

I hang back,
not planning to
talk to anyone. But
Cloudan walks over
to me.

    "This is so embarrassing,"
    he says.

"I mean . . . it's not
a bad thing to
be good at
acting. I think
you have to be
smart to do it.

I know I can't."

"Right, but how important
is that skill? Don't we
need scientists
and doctors
and engineers
more?

People who
keep our
community
running.

So we can stay alive."

I don't like acting.
But that doesn't mean
it's not important.

I think about
Neptune's brother's
mural. The comfort
it brings her.
How Mercury
risked his life
to finish it.

"I think we
need art to
survive too,"
I say.

NEPTUNE

HEY RAINY,

Sending another message
because I forgot to
answer your second question.

I used to be
really annoyed
that my brother could
paint so well
and I couldn't.

All I can do
is make videos
with my dad's old camera!

But now that
Mercury is gone,
I don't feel like that
anymore.

Are you asking because
you're jealous
of your sister?

You don't seem
all that confident
in yourself.

~Neptune

RAINY

DEAR NEPTUNE,

Of course I'm
jealous of my sister.

Snowy is smarter
than me.
She gets perfect scores
on all her tests
and spends hours
talking about math with Dad.

She's prettier
than me.
She was named
for her beautiful, bright
white hair.

She's better at
making friends.
Her best friends
are Skylar and
Electra, but
she gets along
with everyone.

But most of all,
she's not scared of people
the way I am.

~Rainy Donovan

DEAR RAINY,

I heard that there are
fewer than 150 people
on Mars right now.

It makes sense
to have a hard time
with people
when there are so few.

But if you ever come
to Earth,
you'll definitely
find your people.

Except that you'll
probably get
some wild Earth
disease. Then die
before you
make any friends.

Sorry, I'm
being morbid.

My school
closed down
because we
had an outbreak
of raccoon flu.
Which is basically
the flu but it jumped from
raccoons to humans.

Did you know
that could happen?

We'll probably
be back in school
in a couple of days.
I don't really get
what's going on,
but I'm bored
and scared.

Do you have
diseases on Mars?
I feel like we get
new ones every day.

My dad says that's what
happens when the world
is ending.

I don’t know if the
world is ending.

But you all must have
gone to Mars
for a reason.

Your morbid alien friend,
Neptune

RAINY

DEAR NEPTUNE,

I'm sorry about
your school.
That must
be really scary.
I hope you
don't get sick.

We definitely don't
have as many
diseases
as you do.

At least not many that
people can catch
from each other.

A few diseases
came with our
parents from
Earth. A few more
came with restocked
supplies.

Everyone still
blames Spencer Riley
—one of our engineers—
for bringing the
common cold
with him from Earth.

But most of our
problems are
because of food
shortages or
glitches
in the dome
climate.

Otherwise, it's
much safer
than Earth.

I know that
your brother
wanted your
family to go
to Mars.

Do you want
the same thing?

Sincerely,
Rainy Donovan

NEPTUNE

WHEN I READ RAINY'S EMAIL

tears well up
in my eyes.

Of *course* I want
to go to Mars.

My brother and I
used to dream about it
as our parents worked
on the project Earth-side.

Of course I *don't* want
to go to Mars.

Earth is my home.
Earth is my brother's
final resting place.

But Mars could be
safe.

Mars could
help me
s u r v i v e.

Mars was my
brother’s dream.

None of this
really matters
though, because
there’s no way
I can get there.

MY FAMILY ISN'T RICH

My parents have
decent jobs.

They're paid
well enough
for what
they do.

We have
a nice
brownstone
in Brooklyn.

We have
enough money
for me to go
to college.

But their money can't
keep us safe from
hurricanes
or plagues.

And who knows if I'll live
long enough to
go to college?

If I'll be able to
work through my migraines
to do anything important
with my life.

That is,
as long as
I stay on Earth.

JUST TO WALK TO SCHOOL

I have to slap
sunscreen
all over my
body.

Put on
sunglasses
that block
out as much light
as they can
without blinding me.

Put on a hat
made of material
that's supposed to
deflect the sun.

Fill up a giant
travel cup of water
mixed with electrolyte
powder.

Grab a high-powered
mini-fan. Fully charged.

AND ONE MORE THING

I put Mercury's
old inhaler
in my pocket.

The inhaler is empty.
And I don't
have asthma.

It's a good luck charm.
It makes me feel
like I can survive
the brutal heat.

THE PROTEST

The street is
flooded with
people. It's
hard to move.

I don't
want to be late
for school.
I try to walk
around the crowd.

But the crowd
is everywhere.
As thick as fog.

So I give up.
I start reading
the signs
held by
protestors.

Shut Down the Mars Program

Earth Comes First

No Food for Traitors

Only Cowards Go to Mars

I walk up
to the woman
who is holding up
the cowards sign.

“Can you
explain your
sign?” I ask.

The woman
pushes her
curly brown hair
behind her ear.

She says,

“Leaving Earth instead
of staying to help
fix its problems
is cowardly. Humans
caused global warming.

We have to accept
responsibility
for our actions.

We can’t just
run away to
another planet
and ruin it all
over again.”

I FROWN

Mercury
didn't cause
the pollution
that gave him
asthma. He
didn't cause
the extreme
heat that
triggered
his asthma
and killed him.

He wasn't
a coward
for dreaming
of Mars.

He deserved
to be safe.

He didn't deserve
to *D I E*.

I TRY TO EXPLAIN THAT

I hold onto
my brother's
inhaler like it's
a protective charm
as I tell the woman
about my brother.

She responds,
"What happened
to your brother
is tragic. But
that's *exactly*
why we have to
stay on Earth.
We have to
create a world
where that
doesn't happen
to anyone else."

"But if my
brother had
been able
to go to Mars,
he would be
alive.

And I don't
think there's
anything he
could have done
to fix the problems
on Earth. Why
should he have
to stay here
and die?"

"Honey," she says.
"The world is bigger
than what you lost.
You'll see that
when you get older."

I hate being
called honey.

"It is—and the
world is bigger
than the Earth,
too," I say.
"That's what
my parents
always tell me.
They work for
the Mars Program."

The woman
looks at me
with a crumpled
expression.

"You should come
to one of our
Earth Justice meetings,"
she says.

"Maybe that will help
you understand
what we stand for.

There's a meeting
this afternoon at
one. You're
welcome to
come."

"I have school," I say.

But I already know
I'm skipping
last period.

I already know
I'm going
to the meeting.

DEAR ALIEN,

Can you tell me
why you think
humans living on Mars
is a good thing?

Sorry, I know
that's weird.

I'm just wondering.

~Neptune

THE MEETING

I walk up
the rickety stairs
of an old building
on the Lower East Side.

The meeting room
has no markings at all.

Inside, the lights
are too bright.
Like tiny suns
burning my eyes.

I sit down
on a folding chair
and look around.

Most people there
are adults. I
feel out of place.

The woman
I met at the
protest walks
up to the microphone
at the front of the room.

Another woman
with long dark hair
and thick black glasses
stands next to her.

"Welcome to
today's Earth Justice
meeting. My name is
Tzippi.

Our goal is to
get the government
to stop investing
in the Mars Program.

You might be
wondering why
we'd want that."

That is a very
good question.

"The Mars Program
was created because
we made Earth
impossible to
live on.

We caused
global warming.
We damaged
the ozone layer.

We used up
natural resources.
We burned fossil fuels.

We caused thousands
of animals to
go extinct.

We created an unequal
society. Some of us
live in beautiful
homes with
air conditioning.
Some of us can
work at home
to avoid the
latest epidemic.
But some of us
live out on the
streets. Some
of us have to
pick fruit in
the hundred-degree
weather while
getting paid
almost nothing.

Is that fair?"

THE CROWD

They all shake their heads.

And I do too.
Because . . . yeah.
It's *not* fair.

The dark-haired woman
stands up and takes
the microphone.

"I'm Marisol," she says.
She adjusts her glasses.
"It's only the wealthy
and privileged
who get to go
to Mars.

Shouldn't our government
put the money and
manpower it puts
into the Mars Program
into fixing things
here on Earth?"

TZIPPI FINDS ME IN THE CROWD

"Neptune, right?"

But I don't
remember telling
anyone at the
protest my
name.

"Um, yes," I say.

"You said your parents work
for the Mars Program,
sending billionaires
into space.
You said your brother died
because of
climate-related factors.

And I realized—
he's Mercury Rose.
The Mercury Rose."

She faces the crowd.

"You've all seen
his mural in
Brooklyn Bridge Park."

Marisol clicks
to a new slide
on her presentation.

It's a photo of
Mercury's mural.

It's

me.

MY STOMACH TWISTS

I don't like
that they're using
my brother's mural
or his death
to make their points.

Tzippi continues.

"This mural
represents
hope for the future.
Mercury Rose wanted
to go to Mars. He
wanted his little sister
Neptune to go
to Mars. His art
was a symbol
of the movement
to abandon Earth.

But
that was only
because he couldn't
survive on Earth.
He wasn't a champion
of the Mars Program.
He was a *victim*
of the Mars Program."
She turns to me.

"So, Neptune Rose,
will you join our cause?

Will you finish
what your brother couldn't?"

"How can I do that?"
I stammer.

"Finish his mural,"
she says.
"Open the eyes
of all who see it.
Continue his legacy."

MY THROAT GOES DRY

I stare at my feet.
She must sense
my uncertainty.

> "My brother was the artist,"
> I say. "Not me."

"But you're the face
of the mural—
it would draw attention
if you finished it.
It's the perfect way
to show that
what happened
to him was wrong.
That the Mars Program
is wrong."

The audience
roars with
applause.

I want to
disappear.

My parents dedicated their lives
to the Mars Program.

My head starts aching.

When they let me
sit down again,
I wait until
no one is paying
attention to me
and slip out
of the room.

MARISOL FOLLOWS ME OUTSIDE

"Are you okay?" she asks.
"Did we embarrass
you in there?"

"I'm fine," I say,
crossing my arms.

There's a moment
of awkward silence.

"No, you're not,"
she says.
And I realize it's the
first time
someone has said that
out loud to me.

"Okay, I'm *not* fine.
Why did you
ask me to do
that in front
of all those people?
You know I'm only fifteen,
right? Why are
you putting
so much
pressure on me?"

"I'M SORRY"

I'm surprised
by her apology.
She looks like the kind of person
who never apologizes
for anything.

"We shouldn't
have put you on
the spot like that.
It wasn't fair.
But it seems
like you agree
with us. And
your family
makes you
a perfect
symbol for
our movement."

"My brother *believed*
in the Mars Program.
It would be beyond
messed up to
use his art to
say the opposite."

"Do you think
he would still
feel that way
if he were
here right now?

Maybe using
his art would
be a good way
to honor him."

"I don't know. He's
not *here*. He's *dead*.
I can't just decide
what he would have felt."

Marisol nods.
"I understand.
So, maybe
you don't
use his art.
But do you
agree with
our cause?
Do you want
to help?"

I rub my temples.

"Yes," I say.
"But I don't
think wanting
to fix things on
Earth means that
going to Mars
is cowardly.

I think we can
fix things on

Earth *and*
work toward
building lives
on Mars.

I don't want
to throw away
my brother's dream."

FIGHTING FOR EARTH

Marisol nods.

"We can drop
the mural idea,"
says Marisol.
"I don't want
to pressure you
into anything
you don't feel
right about.

What *can* you imagine
doing to fight for
Earth?"

I take a minute.
But my brain is pulsing
with pain.
Nothing comes to mind.

"You think about it,"
Marisol says.

She hands me a card
with her number on it
and leaves me alone
in the deadly heat.

THE MIGRAINE KNOCKS ME OUT

for two days.
I can barely do anything
other than exist.

And then when I
come out of the fog,
it hits me.

I CALL MARISOL

"Videos," I say.
"I record and edit
videos, like documentary-style.
I have footage of Mercury's
last mural,
up until the moment
he collapsed.

I can use that, and make videos
about how
messed up
everything is
with this heat wave.

How deadly it is.

I can record
the protests
to spread the
message.

I can create a channel
for it,
spread it around
Mercury's art circles too."

Marisol says,
"Welcome to the
resistance, Neptune."

MY FIRST VIDEO

I want to make
my channel
mine—not
something
Earth Justice
branded.

But soon after
I start brainstorming,
my head hurts again.

I start to feel pressure
to make this perfect,
but I realize
it's better to *do something*
than to do it perfectly.

Don't be negative.
My teacher's words
echo in my head.

And then I get my
channel name.

NEGATIVE NEPTUNE

I hit record
and start talking:

"Welcome to
NegativeNeptune.

I'm Neptune Rose.
My parents work
for the Mars Program.

I think it's great
that they're helping
to create a new
home for humanity . . .
but that doesn't mean
we can just
give up on fixing
Earth. Because we
can't take everyone
to Mars—and
everyone deserves
a safe home.

On this channel, I'm
going to talk about
all of the things
that make life
on Earth the worst.

I'm not going to
sugarcoat it. I
hate it here. I
want to go to Mars because
maybe if it's not
a million degrees
for half the
year, my brain
won't explode
from migraines.

I'm not going to
stop speaking the truth
until the people
with money and power
listen to me.

Here's a quick fact
to get us started.

Humans have caused
381,150 species to go
extinct. And those are just
the ones we *know about*.
There could be so *many more*.

Anyway, follow me for more
depressing truths about
life on Earth. I'm out!"

Once I post the video,
I send it to the
Earth Justice group chat.

I send it to Andromeda
and some other kids
in my class.

And I send it
to my alien
pen pal.

RAINY

DEAR NEGATIVE ALIEN,

I just watched your video.

I had no idea
that there were
so many animals
on Earth! It's
so sad that
they all went
extinct like that.

Why didn't they teach us
that in school?

I don't really know
what to say yet.

But stay tuned.

Sincerely,
Awkward Alien

I SPEND EVERY POSSIBLE MOMENT

writing to Neptune.
Even though she's writing
from millions of miles away,
she makes me feel
not so alone.

And she says
I make her feel that way too.

That it's been hard
to hang out with people
in real life
since her brother died.

So we write about everything.

The food that's available.
        (She has so many options!)

The sights and sounds of our communities.
        (Hers seems SO much cooler!)

My social anxiety.
        Her killer migraines.

My issues with my sister.
        Her grief over her brother.

The big stuff
and small stuff
and everything
in between.

I NEED SOME ANSWERS

So I stop by the garden
to see Mom
one day after school.

"You know how
we all got pen pals?" I ask Mom.

"Oh, yes. How is
that going?"

"I got paired with Neptune Rose.
She's really nice. But
she's been telling me
a lot of horrible
things about Earth.

Natural disasters,
extreme heat,
and all these
scary new
diseases.
Is Earth
really that bad?"

My mother pats
my head. She
says, "My dear,
that's why we
left Earth. We

wanted to make
sure humanity
could keep going.
Even if we could
no longer do it
on Earth."

"So, is the plan
to eventually
bring everyone
on Earth to Mars?
Neptune said
that that's
impossible.
Is it?"

Mom takes a breath
and closes her eyes.

"Neptune is right.
Bringing *everyone* to Mars
wouldn't work.

That would
make Mars
just as
dangerous
as Earth is.
One of the
biggest problems
on Earth is
overpopulation.

There are
billions of
people there.
Right now, we
can barely sustain
our own little
community.
We want to bring
more people over, yes.
But not at the expense
of those who are
already here."

"So why
do *we* get
to be here
when so many
other people
have to suffer
on Earth? That
doesn't seem fair."

My mother
pushes my hair back
from my face.

She says, "It's *not* fair.
But it's the way it is.

The first people
have to be
the people
who can keep
this place running.

Which means
scientists
and engineers
and doctors.

And anyone
with enough money
to help fund
the mission."

I don't know how
to make it fair,
either. But I
want to
t r y.

FOREST ENTERS THE GREENHOUSE

His eyes are
so wide that
it looks like
he can
see into
my soul.

And he's chewing
on one of his
dreadlocks.

He makes
a beeping sound
to greet me.

This time,
I beep back.

NEPTUNE TOLD ME

that I needed
to find my people.

I thought it was impossible, but—

here's Forest,
and he's being himself.

So maybe I can too.

He might be weird, but
I think I like that.

I don't have to act
normal
when I'm with him.

I'm not afraid
that he will
judge me.

MY MOTHER KEEPS WORMS

She brought them
from Earth. She
hoped that
they could
transform the
Martian soil
into something
we could use
to grow food.

Forest and I
pour a bucket
of garden clippings
into their tank.

> "That one's name
> is Marcus," says Forest.
> "You name one."

"Oh, okay.
How about . . . Benny?
That was my
uncle's name. I
never met him,
obviously."

> "I picked
> Marcus because
> that was *my* uncle's
> name," says Forest.

We’re quiet for a moment.
It’s weird, not knowing
anyone we’re
related to. Except
our parents and
siblings.

Everyone else
was left behind
on Earth. Which
means that they’re
living like Neptune.

LIFE ON EARTH

"Hey Forest?" I ask
as I stir the
garden clippings
into the soil.
"Has your
pen pal told you
much about life
on Earth?"

"Mmmm . . . not
really," he says.
"We mostly
talk about video
games. He sent
me some files
that I can use
to play on
my mom's
terminal.

You should
come over
and play
sometime."

I want to
try Earth
video games.

But the idea
of spending
time in someone
else's home
scares me.

"Um, maybe," I squeak.

I PRESS ON

"My pen pal, Neptune,
told me how dangerous
things are on Earth."

Forest shrugs.
"It's just never
really come up."

"Do you tell him
anything about
life on Mars?"

"Nah, Deimos
doesn't care
about that."

"Okay. Well . . . could
you try asking him
a bit more about
life on Earth?"

FOREST SHRUGS

He pours the
last of the
garden clippings
into the worm tank.

“Maybe later.
Deimos has
raccoon flu.”

That makes me
nervous. I don’t
want Neptune
to get raccoon flu.

We’re just starting
to feel like
friends.

REALITY CHECK

Hearing about
Deimos's illness
makes the things
that Neptune said
feel even more real.

I don't know what
raccoon flu does.

But it proves how
dangerous
Earth really is.

A CRAZY IDEA

Suddenly, I think:
What if I could save
Neptune
from Earth?

What if I could get her here,
where she could live
headache-free
in our dome?

I'd finally have
a real friend
on this planet.

FOREST'S MOTHER IS OUR MAYOR

If anyone
could tell me
how to get
our pen pals
to Mars, it's her.

Nervously, I tell Forest,
"Okay, I'll come
over to your house."

He stares at me.
Unblinking.

"To play video games?"

"Um. Yes."

THE MAYOR'S HOUSE

looks exactly like
all the other
houses in
the dome.

We don't have
the resources
for anything
that sets the
important
people apart.

Forest windmills
his arms as he
walks into
the living room.

> "Maaaaaa," he says.
> "I'm home. I brought
> Rainy."

THE MAYOR

Destiny Redding
looks up from her
terminal.

Usually,
she wears dresses
with prints of
things from
Earth I've never
seen. Cheetahs.
Pomegranates.
Greyhound dogs.

Her hairstyle
changes often
—last time I saw
her, she wore
a braided crown.

She has such a *presence*.

Usually it intimidates me
into silence.

BUT TODAY

her hair
is loose,
and she's
wearing a
pink bathrobe.

"Forest, what did I tell you
about bringing
people over
without asking
me first?" she says.

He shrugs.

"Oh, um, I'm sorry!
I'll leave!"
I turn around
and start heading
for the door.

"No, Rainy,
come back," says
the mayor, sighing.
"You look like you have
something to say."

"Oh. Okay.
Sorry. Um.
Can I ask you something?"

THE BIG QUESTION

"How possible
would it be
to bring
more people
from Earth
to live here?"

She looks surprised
by my question.
Then takes a moment
to figure out how to answer.

"It would be
expensive," she admits.
"The first mission
cost nearly
a trillion dollars.
It's cheaper
now, but a ticket
on a shuttle costs
at least a million dollars.
Not to mention
how much it
would cost
to house and feed each person
for the rest of their life here."

I scratch
the inside of
my wrist.

And bite
my lip.

“So . . . if someone
had enough money,
they could come?”

“Maybe . . . why
do you
want to know?”

Forest, who is
lying upside down
on the couch
chirps, “She found out
that Earth sucks
and our pen pals
are going to die.”

The mayor looks rattled.

Quickly, she asks,
“Who wants a snack?”
and leaves us alone.

HOW CAN I GET A MILLION DOLLARS?

I have no idea.
I have never
earned money
in my life.

It feels impossible.
I feel stupid
for even
mentioning this
to someone as
important as
the mayor.

JUST EXISTING

We are not deterred
by snacks.

Forest starts chewing
on one of his dreadlocks
as we figure out
the money problem.

“I need to chew on
something when
I’m thinking,” he explains.

He pulls out a silicone necklace
from his shirt
and chews on that instead.

I’m starting to love
how unapologetically
weird Forest is.

It makes me
feel like
I’m allowed
to exist too.

I KEEP COMING BACK TO

the NegativeNeptune
channel.

Neptune is using it
to call attention
to things on Earth.

What if *we* made videos
about our lives here?

Answering questions,
like the ones Neptune asked
about our elections.

Giving tours of our space.

We could monetize the videos,
work toward the million-dollar goal.

I tell Forest my idea,
and he says,
“That could
work. Let’s do it.”
I have never been so scared
or so determined
in my life.

WE NEED STAR POWER

We need someone
like Snowy or Electra
to be the face
of the channel.

It pains me to
ask them.

But Neptune
is worth it.

MY PITCH

"If we make enough money,
we could get my pen pal
here," I say
to my sister
and her friends.

"What's so special about *your*
pen pal?" Snowy asks.

"Well, she's really smart and honest,
and she's got these debilitating migraines
because of the heat,
and—"

"I want *my* pen pal to come too,"
says Electra.

And they tell their friends,
and suddenly everyone
is on board Project Pen Pal.

MY SISTER

is *thrilled*
to be on camera.
Electra wants to be
in the videos too.

Cloudan offers
his dad's recording equipment.

If there's one thing
the Mars kids
know about,
it's pitching in with
a group project.

I'm not sure
what I've gotten myself
into.

THE WU HOUSE

is nothing like
the mansion
they lived in
on Earth.

From the outside,
it looks exactly
like every other
house.

But inside,
it's one
of the nicest
houses in
the dome.

The perfect backdrop
for our first episode.

It's time to
get to work.

OUR CHANNEL IS CALLED "FIRST-GEN MARTIANS"

It's not the most
creative name.
But Mr. Wu says
it's more important
to be clear than
creative.
And he's letting us
use this channel
as our final project
for his class!

Skylar has been
watching makeup
tutorials. She
got a big box of
makeup in our
last delivery from
Earth. So she's
doing everyone's
makeup.

"Me? No," I say,
pushing away the makeup.
I have never
worn makeup
before.

I don't want anyone
to see me wearing it.
I don't want anyone
to have thoughts
about how I look.

But Skylar
insists,
"You've got to be
part of this too."

"It was *your* idea,"
Snowy agrees.

So I let them
make me up.

Just this once.

OUR FIRST VIDEO

Features a tour
of the greenhouse.

Snowy says
that Earth kids
are *fascinated*
by how we live.

Even the most normal thing
to us is alien to them.

So Snowy and I
interview our mom
about growing food on Mars.

Before we start,
Mom says,
“Pretend there
isn’t a camera.
You’re
just hanging out
in here with me.
Like you always do.”

> “How do you decide
> what to grow?” I whisper.
> Directing my voice
> at my shoes.

"Speak *up*," hisses Snowy.

So I try my best.

DEAR POSSIBLY EVENTUAL MARTIAN,

I don't know if
you've seen
our videos.

I'm in a few of them.
Kinda useless
in front of the camera,
I know.

Snowy says
we're not going to get any views
with me standing
around talking to my shoes.

But the videos
are getting tons of views!

We're going to
use the money
to help sponsor
people who
want to move to Mars.

I want you to know—
you're first on our list.
I wish I could do more.

Your Determined Alien Friend,
Rainy

DEAR RAINY,

I am in shock
right now.
Are you serious?!

First of all, thank you
SO MUCH. You
did NOT have to
do all that!!

Second of all, you
are doing something
useful. You were great
in those videos.

And you decided I should be
one of the people to get
a ticket. That means so much.

Why do you think that
you're useless?
I don't get it.

I'll help you
work on that
when I get
to Mars.

Your biggest alien fan,
Neptune

I SHOW RAINY'S LETTER TO MY MOTHER

She sighs.
Doesn't talk
for a long time.

"Baby," she says.
"This is such a
sweet thing for
your pen pal
to do. But
it's not
realistic.

They probably
won't be able
to make enough
money through
videos alone.

Even if they can . . .
A ticket isn't
enough to build
a life.
It's a billionaire's dream,
not ours."

I don't reply,
so Mom keeps
talking.

"Plus, it takes six months to
get to Mars.
You get
antsy
when you
have to be
on the subway
for an hour."

My mother
leans over
the kitchen counter.
Tries to take
my hand.

I snatch it away.

"Mercury wanted
me to go to Mars.

Isn't that a good
enough reason
to take the risk?"

"No," she says.
"I already lost
my son.
I can't lose
my daughter too."

"YOU WON'T LOSE ME"

I promise.
"I'll talk to you
all the time.
And when the
prices go down,
I'll visit."

"That's if you get
to Mars in the first
place. The shuttles
aren't as
stable as the
public thinks they
are. Some of the
ships that were
sent to Mars never
made it there.

Besides, once
you get there . . .
it's the wilderness.
They rely on a single
greenhouse to
feed 150 people.
They have only
one doctor and
they don't have
advanced medicine.

That's important,
Neptune. You
need access to
good medical
care if you don't
want your migraines
to get worse."

"That's part
of why I
want to
go. If I'm
somewhere
with temperature
control, I won't
get nearly as
many migraines."

"You don't *know* that.
And even if that's
true, there are
all kinds of
dangers you
haven't considered.

Honestly, I think
it will be a miracle
if they make it
past the next
generation."

“It’ll be a
miracle if
Earth lasts
that long!

It’s going to be
125 degrees
outside tomorrow.

We’ll probably
have another
blackout like
we always do.
That means
no air conditioner
and no air filters.

I’m going to spend
the whole time with
eighty migraines
stacked on top
of each other.

I know it’s not
fair that I might
be able to leave
and others can’t.

But I don’t want
to die here.”

"You'd rather die
in space, millions
of miles away
from anyone
who loves you?"

"You could
come with me!"

"No. I can't leave
the place where
my son
is buried.

I'm sorry, baby.

This just isn't
going to work."

I'm not ready
to give up
completely.

SINCE I CAN'T GO TO MARS

I go to another protest.

This time, I'm
not just watching.

I'm recording. I'll
blur their faces
later—Tzippi
and Marisol
told me that
it is really
important
to protect
identities.

Their signs say
things like *"Shut
down the Mars
Program and
start Universal
Health Care."*

and

*"Why send rich
people to Mars
when you could
be fixing global
warming?"*

I don't think
they understand
the hope
that Mars
represents.

But why should they?
They will probably
never have a
chance to
go there.

Mars won't
be ready for
more than a
handful of people
for centuries.

People need
things *now*.

If Mercury
had had the
things on
their signs,
he wouldn't
have needed
to dream
about Mars.

He'd still be
alive.

When I finish
filming, I grab a sign
from Tzippi's
stash. It's blank.

Using a red marker,
I write
a message
I think
I believe in.

> *"Mars is the future,
> but don't let
> Earth become
> the past."*

WEEKS PASS BY

in a stream
of recording and
posting videos,

watching our followers
rise from
100 to 1,000
to 100,000
to 1,000,000.

Watching our profits rise too.
Earth celebrities chip in!
We are getting so close to covering
the first ticket.

I plug Neptune's channel,
and she supports mine.
We write to each other
nearly every day,
with updates
and encouragement.

The other pen pals
have been getting close too.

It makes us work
even harder.

MAYOR REDDING

stops by our class,

We're working on
editing videos.
We're on a roll!

The one I'm
working on
explains that
Mars has the
biggest volcano
in the solar system.

It's called Olympia Mons.
It's 14 miles tall, and
it's as wide as
the state of Arizona.

I don't know how
big Arizona is, but
Ms. Nazarian
said people on
Earth would
understand.

After watching us
for a few minutes,
Mayor Redding
walks to the front
of the classroom.

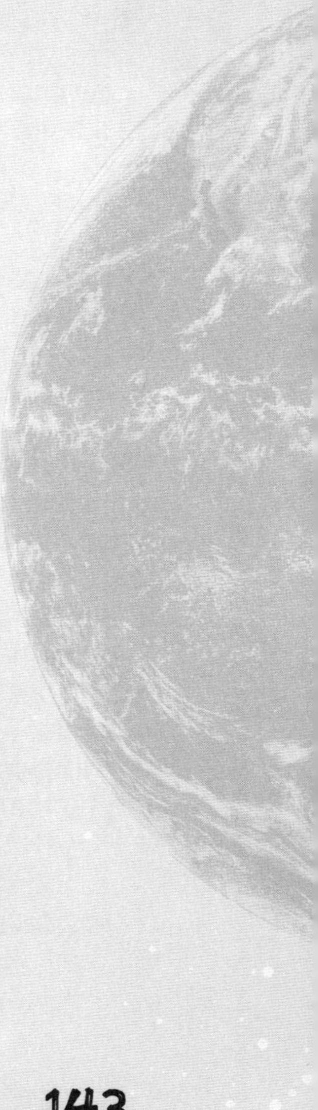

"Hi kids!" she says.
She sounds a
little too cheerful.

"It's great to
see you working
hard on your
new channel.
It's been
extremely
successful.

I can't believe
you were able
to start making
money so fast!"

She pauses. Her
smile is too bright
and too wide.

"We're going to have
a town hall meeting
to discuss the project
tonight.
I'd love for all of you
to be there."

THE TOWN HALL MEETING

is in our community center.
All our parents,
the scientists and engineers,
are there.

Mayor Redding
opens by addressing our channel.
We cheer.
We've gotten so many views,
raised so much money.

It all seems possible
right now.

She clears her throat.
"Yes, great job, kids!
But I just wanted to
explain something.

I know you're
all excited to
share your
lives with your
pen pals. But
some of you
have been
talking about
wanting to
bring your
pen pals to
Mars.

This is *very* sweet.

And you might
be able to
afford a few
tickets. But
we can't just
take *anyone*.

If we offer
anyone a
ticket on
the Mars Shuttle
and a place in our community,
they're going to
have to be
useful."

My heart slams
against my
ribs. I don't
even know what
Mayor Redding
is going to say. But
I already feel
like I've failed.

"This means that
your channel
can help them
with money for a trip.

But it’s a long journey
for a short visit.
It would be even more
complicated
to allow them to *stay*.”

“So it’s impossible,” I say,
my heart feeling
defeated.

The mayor looks sympathetic
as the kids start to
mutter and groan.

Snowy stands up.
“So the Mars Program
is just for a privileged few.
Everyone else just, what?
Dies on Earth?”

Mayor Redding’s face
flushes.
“I’m saying we have to be
extremely selective.”

THE MEETING EXPLODES

Everyone is
yelling at the
same time. I
want to put my
hands over my
ears and hide.

Electra says, "Why
are we doing all
this work if we'll
never actually
save our pen pals?"

Stratta folds her
hands and frowns
hard. Skylar yells
that the mayor is
being *mean*.

Snowy says, "Forest,
why is your mom
betraying us?"

"Mom, why are you
betraying us?" asks
Forest, his voice flat.

SOMETHING TO SAY

I am usually
the quiet one.

The awkward one.

On the outside
of any conversation.

But I have something to say,
and I stand up.

“Mayor, I wish you would
have told us this
earlier. Before we even
met our pen pals.
Instead of keeping it
from us.
Our whole lives,
we were told the Mars Program
was the most important project
for humanity.
But it only helps a few humans.
We are the lucky ones.”

Everyone looks
at me like I have
seven heads. My
face boils with
embarrassment.

But I keep talking.

"I get that we can't bring
billions of people here.
But there has to be some
chance that it could happen
for people.

We can't survive without
the Earthians.

We are *not* self-sustaining.

We need each other."

Mayor Redding
nods her head
like she's listening
and agreeing with me.

But I have no plan
for a path forward.

And the meeting ends.

DEAR NEPTUNE,

Sorry I haven't written much
this week.

The other Martians and I
have been hard at work.

Forest and I
made a video
about our worm farm
that somehow got
10 *million* views.

We're so close
to our first goal.

Your hopeful alien,
Rainy

MY HEART BREAKS

reading Rainy's message.
She's trying so hard
to get me to Mars.
How can I tell her
that my parents said no?

Before I
can reply,
the screen goes dark.

It's not just my
terminal —
it's every
terminal
and every light
in the room.

"I'll look for
the circuit breaker,"
says Milkiwei.

I look out
into the
school hallway.

It's not just
the Terminal Room.

All the lights in
the hallway
are dead.

The rest of the
classrooms
have gone
dark too.

IT'S NOT JUST THE LIGHTS

The air conditioning
has gone out.

If it doesn't
come back
on soon,
the building
will turn into
a broiler.

OUTSIDE THE WINDOW

I see pouring
rain.

Mr. Okafor
steps into
the hall, saying,
“Everyone, get
your things.
We are evacuating
the building.

We’re going to
a shelter at the university.
Your parents have
been informed.”

THE HURRICANE

When I
get outside,
I understand
why the power
went out.

The sky is
d a r k.

It's
p o u r i n g
rain.

The wind is
s c r e a m i n g.

I can't hear
the sound of a
tree
s n a p p i n g
in half over
the sound
of t h u n d e r.

"The news said
this hurricane
wasn't going
to hit New York,"
says Mr. Okafor.

We all pile
onto school
buses
and speed
toward
the shelter.

THE SHELTER IS CROWDED

There isn't room for
the whole school
to stay together.

I realize that there are
more people in here
than in the whole Mars Colony.

The teachers
divide us
up.

I grab Andromeda's
hand so we stick together.
It's slick
with rain
and sweat.

I regret avoiding her
these last few months.

I realize we all
need one another—

especially now.

THE GENERATOR

The shelter's generator
is working for now.

That means
air conditioning.
But it might
not last.

If it fails,
we will have to
face the 125-degree
heat. It will be
worse than
at school
because there
are thousands
of other people
here.

Deimos takes a puff
from his inhaler.

I shudder.

If he's
already having
trouble breathing,
he won't survive
when the
heat closes in.

Didn't he
just get over
raccoon flu?
He's in even more
danger than
Mercury had
been.

I don't want to
watch my friend
          d i e
like my
brother
did.

Andromeda
catches me watching.

"He's fine," she says.
"He'll be fine.
This isn't
going to be
like Mercury."

          "I know. I know.
          I just. I can't
          handle it if—"

"You have to
keep yourself
calm. And he's
going to be
okay. We all are."

BUT THERE ISN'T ENOUGH FOOD

for everyone at
the shelter.

I receive
a cheese sandwich
in a plastic bag.

Also,
a banana.

I hate
both of those
things.

But the shelter
employee
who gives them to me
says that I'm
lucky to get
anything at all.

I should be
grateful. But
all I can
think about
is how
much I
want to
leave.

THE DOOR BURSTS OPEN

A crowd of adults
files into the shelter.
My parents
are among them.

They're both panting
and gasping. Soaked
from the rain.

"Mom! Dad!" I shout.
Waving my arms
so that they
see me.

They jog toward me.
My father wraps
his arms around
my shoulders.

"Neptune," he says.
His voice is soft
like bruised fruit.

"We have some
bad news."

THE BAD NEWS

is that
our home
has been
destroyed.

The wind
ripped a tree
from its roots.
Launched it straight
through the front
of our brownstone.

“Nobody got hurt,”
says Mom.
“But we won’t
be able to go
home for
a while.”

“Where will we stay?”
I bite my lip.

“At the shelter,
for now,” says Dad.
“After that, we might
be able to stay
with my sister
in Alabama, but
the heat is
so much
worse there.

Plus, the tornados
there are as bad
as our hurricanes—
maybe worse."

"But it's okay," says Mom.
"We'll figure it out.
We're all alive.
That's what matters."

WHAT MATTERS

I film the shelter
while I wait
for my parents
to figure out
where we're
going next. This
is going on
my channel.

"Hey everybody,
it's Negative Neptune.
We had *another*
hurricane. No
surprise—they've
been happening
every few
weeks lately.

This one was
worse than
usual, though.

My house
got destroyed
by a flying tree.

Andromeda, tell
us what happened
to your apartment."

“My mom says
that the first four
floors of the building
are filled with
sewer water.
We live on
the third floor.”

“Gross! Just in case
people don’t know,
sewer water can
contain E. coli and salmonella.
It can cause shigellosis,
typhoid fever,
and cholera.

So yeah, thanks a lot
corporations who are
ruining the environment—
thanks to you, a teenage
girl’s apartment
is filled with
bacteria.”

NEPTUNE DOESN'T ANSWER MY LETTERS

But it's not just me. Nobody
hears from their pen pals.
We don't know why.

Snowy thinks that
maybe their terminal system
went down.

Electra thinks
maybe they
got hit by
a meteor.

I think that
maybe they all
decided they
hate us and
want nothing
to do with us.

But maybe I'm
wrong. I think
that's just my
brain being mean to me.

That's what Neptune would say.

AN ALERT GOES OFF

for the NegativeNeptune channel,
and I watch my pen pal
interviewing people
at a shelter.

There's been a hurricane.

She could have died!

She's *homeless*.

I wish I could save her,
right now.

I feel so useless.

NEPTUNE

DEAR HURRICANE-FREE ALIEN,

Sorry for not getting
back to you.

I don't know
if you heard,
but we just
went through
a hurricane.

I just spent
about a week
in a shelter.

Our house got hit
by a tree. So
now we're in
a hotel for
a couple of
days while
my parents
figure out
what to do.

They're spending
most of their time
on the phone. Yelling
at insurance companies.

Do you have insurance
companies on Mars?

I guess I'll find out soon
because guess *what??*

My parents said
I can accept the
offer!!

Listen—this
wouldn't have
happened
without you.

The videos were *your* idea,
and *your* video
is the one that
made the most money.

I think
this is proof
that you *do*
have talent.
And you *are*
worth listening to.

I can't wait to
meet you in person.

Your Future Martian Friend,
Neptune

THE CALL

I'm about to sign out
of the Mars terminal,
when I see a call
coming through.

"Rainy?!"

"Oh, um, hi,"
Rainy says,
looking like she's
fighting off tears.

"Hi!"
It feels so good
to see her.
The time differences
between us are always
so crazy.
We've never tried
to call before.

"Are you okay?"
she asks, with a frown.

"I'm safe,"
I assure her.
"I'm okay."

She looks relieved.

Then she says,
"Please—please don't hate me."

"What's going on?"
I ask.

She looks away and says,
"I have good news
and bad news."

WE SPEND TWO HOURS

on the video call
trying to come up with solutions
to the Mars Program
problem.

They almost have
the money for a shuttle ticket!

But the Colony doesn't want
more people to live there.
And she hasn't been able
to find a solution.

We come up with so many ideas:

An Earth-Mars exchange program
(temporary and expensive).

A dome expansion project
(*crazy* expensive).

Sneaking onto Mars as a "visitor"
and just refusing to leave
(super illegal).

Finally, we land on something.

Turns out,
we're a really good
team.

WHAT IF

I run all the way
to Forest's house,
just in time to see
Mayor Redding
getting in her golf cart.

"Rainy! Good to see you,"
she says with a smile.

"You too," I say,
out of breath.

"Something on your mind?"

"You mentioned that
anyone who lives on Mars
needs to be useful to Mars.
And we're doing okay right now.
But what happens when our
specialists retire?"

"That's what you kids are for,"
she laughs.

I shake my head.
"There aren't enough of us here
to fill the roles.

We will need Earthians.

What if we made a college scholarship
for people willing to learn
a specific trade needed on the colony?"

Mayor Redding
takes a moment
to think about this.

"This would mean
your pen pals wouldn't be able
to come over for a few years,"
she says.
"They'd need adequate training
in a predetermined field."

"That's okay," I say.
"It's still a chance.
It's still hope.
Sometimes all people need
is hope."

"I'll talk to the Program's
board," she promises.
"Good thinking, Rainy."

And because I know
Neptune would want me to,
I take the praise.

OUR FIRST MILLION

I can hardly believe it
when our videos
finally earn
enough money
for a ticket to Mars.

We have a party
at the Wu's House.

They serve rehydrated
Dan Dan noodles
and freeze-dried
ice cream cake
that they brought
from Earth.

My mom brings
strawberries and
pea shoots from
the garden.

Mayor Redding
even shows up.

"You kids are
something else,"
says Mayor
Redding as she
pets the top
of Forest's head.

"If you're going to
pet me like a cat,
I will meow like one,"
he says. "MEOW."

I can't help laughing.

These past few months,
Forest has become
my best friend on Mars.

SOMETHING GOOD

Mayor Redding says,
"I'm glad you're having
a good time, Rainy.
The video that
you and Forest
made about
the worm farm
was the biggest
hit on the channel.

You two did great.
Everyone, you
should give
these two
a round of
applause!"

I am shocked
to see everyone
clapping. Not
just the adults
who always
clap when
the kids
do something.

Electra. Snowy.
People who
usually think
I'm a useless idiot
think I did
something good.

Wait—
I *did* do something
good.

And it feels good
to have them
say so.

Turns out,
I'm not useless
after all.

FOREST TAKES MY HAND

and makes me bow
with him.

It's so fast that
the blood rushes
to my head.

Mayor Redding
smiles at Stacy
and Lance.

"The Wu Family
has agreed to
match what
you earned."

Mr. Wu says,
"And we're all working
on a partnership
with a few
Earth universities
so that new people
can get the training
they need to
work here."

“With luck, we’ll
be able to start
bringing a new team
over within a few
years,” says
Mayor Redding.

“For now, we’ll be
drawing up
contracts and
offering them
to whoever
we think
has potential.

But because
you kids
worked
so hard,
we’re going
to let you
choose
who you
want to
offer the
first two
contracts
to. After that,
it’ll be an
application
process.”

IT'S USUALLY HARD TO ASK FOR WHAT I WANT

But this is worth
speaking up for.

"Neptune Rose,"
I say, firmly. "If that's
okay with everyone
else, I mean."

"Of course it is!"
snaps Snowy.
"You get to pick,
remember?"

She says it with an edge.
But I know that it's just
because she wants me
to see this through.

Maybe Neptune is right.
Maybe my sister does care about me.

"Um," I say.
"Okay. I choose Neptune."

FOREST CHOOSES DEIMOS

Nobody is surprised.

Deimos is the one he
plays video games
with and never talks
to about what life
is like on Earth.

Mayor Redding
reminds us that
this is just
an offer.

If they don't
accept, or
their parents
don't agree,
the offer
will go to
someone
else.

AN OFFER I CAN'T REFUSE

When the official offer
arrives from the Mars Program,
I can hardly believe it.

My mom tears up.
She doesn't want me to leave,
but she's happy
I have the opportunity.

My dad thinks it's *so cool*
and can't wait
to have a Martian daughter.

NOW I JUST HAVE TO . . .

get through
three more years
of high school

and two years
of college
training in interplanetary
agricultural
science.

While battling
the heat
and the migraines.

But I have to do this—
for Mercury.

And for myself.

STILL, SOMETHING FEELS WRONG

about going
to a safe planet
when my fellow humans
are stuck here.

Rainy and I decide to have
weekly meetings
to discuss the direction
of our channels,
how the proceeds will be spent,
and how I can best
give back
to my home planet.

We decide
to spend any extra money
on climate research
and sustainable air conditioning systems
for lower-income populations
around the world.

We can't save Earth.

But that doesn't mean
we can't make
some
small
difference.

UNTIL I LEAVE

I'll keep filming,
and telling the story
of the people on Earth
who need help.

The protests of people
who want change.

I'll lift up the dreams
of the people
in the streets,

and continue
my brother's legacy.

THE MURAL

I'm not the artist
in the family,

but my brother *did*
teach me a few things.

And I want to
finish his mural.

There's my own hand
reaching up to
Mars,
the last thing
he painted.

And then I paint
a hand reaching back
from Mars to Earth.

I hope everyone
gets the message:

If any of us
are going to survive,
we've got to
help
each
other.

RAINY

I'M BUSY THESE DAYS

Filming with my sister
and *our* friends.

Hanging out with Forest
and our worms.

But I always stop by the terminal
to write to Neptune
before I start
my day.

DEAR ALIEN,

It's kinda weird
to have a best friend
who lives on a different planet.

But good news!

Just 2,000 more days
until you can
join us here
on Mars.

I know it's
going to be a long
time, but our letters
keep me going.

And I know you're
going to do great
things while
you're on
Earth.

And when you get here,
we're going to do
great things—
together.

Yesterday, my
dad told me
that Earth
has sunsets

that are orange,
pink, and purple.

Ours are blue. Yours
sounds beautiful.
But I think
you'll really
love the sunset here.

The blue is the
same color
Mercury used
in the background
of his mural.

You'll have to see it
yourself
when you get here.

Until then,
your Martian friend

WANT TO KEEP READING?

If you liked this book, check out another book from West 44 Books:

THE SOULMATE PROJECT

BY ANNA LINDWASSER

ISBN: 9781978598355

THE 2065 SOULMATE APPLICATION

has so many
pointless questions.

Some of them
are annoying,
and some of them
make me angry.

Why are there so many
about what I look like?
What I want my
partner to look like?

Aren't there other
things that are more
important than that?

Like personality?
Or opinions, goals, hobbies?

I think I'm beautiful.
Nobody will see my picture
and have any problems—
at least, not anyone
with good taste.

But I don't want
to be judged
for my looks
alone.

I don't want
some jerk
who thinks
my crossed eyes
are ugly
to get the chance
to turn me down.

None of that
matters. Because
my boyfriend and I
are lying to get matched.

THIS
TRAUMA
IS SPONSORED
LIVE
Anna
Lindwasser

TROUBLE
ON THE
SOLAR
WIND
DEMITRIA LUNETTA

THE
FINAL
DIADEM

THE LAST
STAR
CHASER
Demitria Lunetta

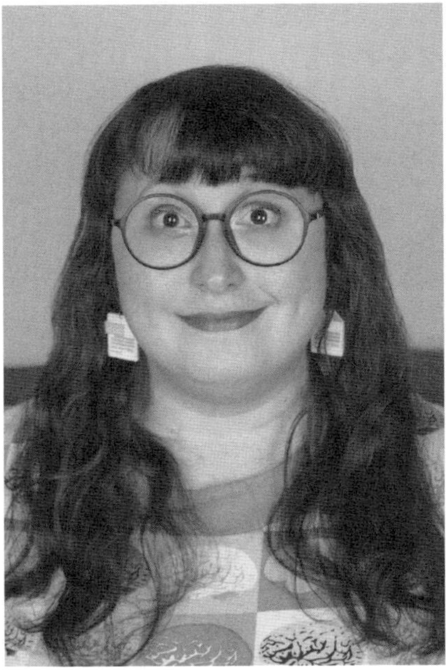

ABOUT THE AUTHOR

Anna Lindwasser is an MFA candidate at the University of Alabama. She spends her days reading, writing, and teaching college students. In a past life, she taught ELA and creative writing to high school and middle school students in New York City. When she isn't working, she can be found looking for birds she's never seen before or making playlists about her characters. *Dear Alien is* her third work of hi-lo fiction.